GRANDMA'S WEDDING QUILTS

THE PREQUEL

A Sweet & Clean Prequel to the Multi-author Sweet Americana Club Series, Grandma's Wedding Quilts

By Kate Cambridge

GRANDMA'S WEDDING QUILTS
THE PREQUEL
A Sweet & Clean Prequel to the Multi-author Sweet
Americana Club Series, Grandma's Wedding Quilts
By Kate Cambridge
SIGN UP FOR KATE CAMBRIDGE'S CHOICE READER UPDATES FOR LATEST
NEWS, GIVEAWAYS, SPECIAL BOOK LAUNCH PRICING, AND MORE!
VISIT KATECAMBRIDGE.COM/CHOICE

Be sure to check out all the books in the Grandma's Wedding Quilts Series. The links to
all the books can be found at the end of this book.
Kate Cambridge is a bestselling Amazon author, writing both Sweet Historical Romance
and Sweet Contemporary Romance books
.
Visit KateCambridge.com

Table of Contents

CHAPTER 1:

There it was, that musty smell that filled Hannah Quinn with excitement. It was the same aroma that drifted off the pages of books that hadn't been opened in centuries. To her, it signaled an opportunity to time travel, a chance to obtain knowledge that might have been lost for hundreds of years, a story waiting to be told.

Only today, it drifted from the surface of an old trunk. It wasn't the oldest thing she'd ever laid eyes on, not by far, but it was interesting. The trunk itself was quite large, and heavy. It had likely traveled across open seas along with immigrants from another country. With its faint scuff marks and worn latches, it whispered a story about being moved, and used, throughout the years. It wasn't just tucked away, at least not at first; it was an important part of someone's household, perhaps several households.

"Can I touch it?"

"Sure, Hannah, it's already been processed and ready to be opened. Just be gentle with the latches; they're so old they might break off. In light of the fact that we don't know what's inside, it could be the trunk that holds value."

"I'll be careful, Sheena, ugh… Dr. Wagstaff."

"Let's open it, Hannah," she sighed, peering at her assistant over the top of her glasses. "I know you can't wait."

Hannah smiled and ran her fingers over the smooth, dusty surface of the trunk. The moment she touched it, a sense of warmth filled her and made her shiver at the same time. She had the feeling that this trunk was very loved, and that its contents would be just as sentimental. A part of her hoped it would hold some expensive antique, as the museum was under pressure to come up with funds to stay open. But her instincts and experience told another story. This was a family heirloom, something passed from parent to child for decades.

The detailed brass work and latches were exquisite, and scratches on the corners suggested it had once been stored somewhere tight. Maybe mounds of belongings had been piled around it and on top of it. Maybe in an attic, maybe in a basement, maybe in an old storage room. Now, magically, it was right in front of her, and Hannah couldn't wait to find out why.

"Do you have any information about who donated it?"

"Yes, we have the paperwork; it came with a few other things, as well. It sounded like it was a clean-out of someone's home and Malcolm believes this holds the most potential value."

Malcolm Siple was in charge of managing donations and gifts to the museum, and his track record regarding the perceived value of donations had often been wrong before, but this wasn't the right time to bring that up. With the museum being tight on funding, there wasn't the money to hire a collections specialist with advanced degrees and experience. And although protocol mandated that all potential donators complete intake forms for consideration at the monthly board meeting, Malcolm was known for bypassing all of that from time to time—if people were willing to sign the Deed of Gift form, transferring ownership to the museum with no regard for monetary value or tax deductions. This was one of those times.

"I wonder what's inside. Did the paperwork say?"

"No. They simply listed the trunk and a few other items on the form. Malcolm said it appeared the donor couldn't wait to just be rid of it. I know you're excited, Hannah, but keep in mind, often linens were stored in trunks like these, at the foot of the bed. Or it could be filled with old newspapers."

"Yes, Dr. Wagstaff," was all Hannah replied. But she had a feeling about this one—and she couldn't let it go. She had learned over the past year of working with Dr. Wagstaff that, although brilliant, she stayed very detached from the items that were donated. Items standardly went into what Hannah fondly thought of as the "Wagstaff Hierarchy of Value"—the last of which being "Space-Filler." Lately, most of the donations had found themselves in that category.

Hannah met Dr. Wagstaff's eyes and she watched resignation filter through them.

"You look like you might burst if I make you wait any longer, Hannah. I do admire your enthusiasm that never seems to dampen, regardless of how many times you go through the accession process. I feel compelled to remind you, though, that the trunk alone may be worth more than anything inside of it."

Hannah watched as the museum director traced the latches, testing them gently, and then surveyed the hinges. "It's actually in decent shape. It may just open right up. Why don't you do the honor?"

"Really? Are you sure?" Hannah asked cautiously.

"You've been my assistant for over a year now, Hannah. I think you know how to open a trunk." She nodded her head. "Just take it easy, open it slowly."

"Okay," she took a deep breath. "Thanks, Dr. Wagstaff." Ever since Hannah had been hired at the museum, she'd worked directly under Sheena Wagstaff, Ph.D. She enjoyed unearthing her colleague's voluminous knowledge as an experienced curator almost as much as she enjoyed learning about the antiques and artifacts that paraded through the walls of the museum. With a gentle touch, Hannah tried to ease the latches open; they resisted, as though comfortable in their current state and unwilling to budge.

With her next breath, she pried them open and lifted the lid of the trunk. It creaked ever so slowly open, and she was greeted by another scent. It was musty, thick, and peppered with perfume. "Wow, look at this, Dr. Wagstaff." She stepped back so that she could see the multi-colored fabric inside of the trunk. "It looks like a quilt, but a unique one. I've not seen this pattern before."

"Just as I suspected, a linen trunk. Not much of value in there," the doctor's voice lilted low, discouraged.

"Oh, but it's gorgeous! Look at the detail in all of these different patches."

"It's beautifully stitched, that's for sure, but quilts are easy to come by, regardless of how old they are. What else does the trunk contain?"

"It looks like there's another quilt, and some household items. A teapot, some silverware, and a little wooden dog."

"Well, it is what it is. The trunk is still a good find, with highly unusual detail."

"I think the quilts are amazing. We should lay them out and take a closer look."

"Sure. You can use the table Malcolm cleaned earlier. But, Hannah, don't get too caught up in them. Let's not forget that we are searching for a way to keep this museum funded, and a couple of quilts aren't going to do that."

"Yes, you're right. I'd just like to see the stitching, and maybe figure out when they were made."

"We need to prioritize, Hannah. Let me know if you find anything interesting. Otherwise, I prefer that you work on the latest list we have from Malcolm and prepare to present on each item at the board meeting next week. We have an exhibit to plan, and it needs to be a success."

Dr. Wagstaff turned to walk away, paused, and turned

back, peering past Hannah into the trunk. "You know, quilts were once used as a way to record family history. Many women would sew in pieces of clothing, tablecloths—some would even weave in locks of hair from their children."

"Really? I knew women often had to reuse fabrics in many forms, but I didn't realize they used hair. That's a little strange; I'm not sure how I missed that detail."

"Time and experience teach us things that often books can't, Hannah. For some, quilting was one way to record memories at a time when many women were not permitted to learn how to read or write. The quilts were often placed on the laps of the elderly, both to keep them warm and to allow them to travel through the memories the quilt contained. Too often now, we rely on technology to store our memories. But if we are no longer lucid enough to work a computer, how will we relive our memories?"

Hannah kept her face passive; moments like these when she caught a glimpse of the human Dr. Wagstaff were few and far between.

"That's a great perspective, Doctor. I'd never looked at it quite like that. I take the tools that I use to catalog and document artifacts and antiques for granted, although part of what I love most about what I do is finding and recreating the story behind the pieces we deem valued enough to trace their past. I imagine it would be very comforting for a woman in her final years to be able to run her fingers along locks of her children's hair, or recall the clothes that they liked to wear, or the meals shared on a particular tablecloth. This makes me even more curious about the stitching on the corner of each of these squares. I look forward to determining if they have significance."

"Maybe they do, Hannah." Dr. Wagstaff smiled, with a tinge of sadness in her eyes. "Just because something has little to no monetary value, doesn't mean that it's not valuable or even priceless to the one who holds it close."

The rise of her eyebrows was involuntary, and Hannah tried to cover it with a cough. "Yes, of course, that is very true." In the next motion, she pulled on some gloves, reached toward the trunk, and ran her hands gently over the top of the quilt. The stitches seemed strong, and even through the gloves she could feel the softness of the fabric, and the variations from the beautifully crafted patterns; it truly was exquisite. When she lifted one corner of the quilt, she was surprised by how heavy it was. More accustomed to the light and fluffy comforters that had always covered her bed, she wondered at the variety of materials that were stitched into the quilt. Some were light and thin like silk, and others were thick and a little rough. Each square was almost exactly the same size, which led her to believe that only one person created the quilt. She likely used one square as her guideline to cut out another.

What was most remarkable to her was that every single square was a different material, yet each beautifully crafted. She'd seen quilts prior to this in the process of her research that contained a single, repetitive pattern, but this quilt appeared to be designed to tell a story, rather than simply accent a space, as so many blankets do today.

On each patch of material, a design had been sewn into

the cloth in the lower right corner. Each square contained a pattern with various shapes and colors. The only similarity was their approximate size. She carried the quilt over to the waiting table and spread it out across the surface. As she smoothed it down, she was enchanted by the embroidered area in the lower corner; to her, they seemed almost like hieroglyphics, an ancient language with a story to tell, yet in all likelihood, they were simply frayed from wear.

"The majority of this quilt is in remarkable condition," Hannah said to no one in particular.

"It must have been in climate controlled environments for some time." Dr. Wagstaff's voice behind Hannah startled her; she was so engrossed in the quilt, she hadn't realized she'd followed her to the table.

"Yes, it must have. What do you think these embroidered areas mean?"

"I have no idea, but that's your project, right?" Dr. Wagstaff raised an eyebrow, "I have some carbon dating to do. Let me know if you find anything of true interest."

After she left the room, Hannah sighed. The old Dr. Wagstaff was back.

She turned back to the trunk to explore the other items. She couldn't wait to examine the second quilt. As she lifted it out, she noticed how different it was from the first. This one had a repeating pattern. Although each square was made of a different material, many of the colors were similar and alternated to create a pleasant design. After staring at it for a few moments, she realized the design was familiar. She settled the quilt back into the trunk and walked over to the first one. As she suspected, an identical design was on one of the large squares of the first quilt.

"What are you trying to tell me?" She smiled as she ran her gloved fingertips over the quilt again. There was no question in her mind that these quilts had a story to tell, and she was going to find out exactly what that was. Although Hannah would never admit this to anyone, she often felt the life of the story behind an item even before her research began. After six years of education, internships, and now a position as assistant director in a prestigious museum, she was beginning to recognize and honor her own intuitive sense when an item held more value than what initially met the eye, and she had yet to find it fail her.

After documenting each of the items in the trunk, she requested the original paperwork from the office and sat down to review it. The donor's name and phone number were listed, but not the address of where the items were found. She dialed the number on the form and hoped someone would pick up.

"Hello." A woman's voice answered, deadpan.

"Delores? Hi, my name is Hannah Quinn. I work for the Nelson-Atwell Museum where you recently donated some items."

"Yes?" Her tone was impatient.

"I was just wondering if you could tell me a little bit about the items that you donated. The trunk contained some beautiful quilts—"

"Yes, I know about the quilts. Trust me." A groan traveled through the phone.

"You do? Great! Could you tell me a little bit about their history?"

"Honestly, I don't know that much about their history. I just know that my mother refused to allow me to get rid of them. Now that she's gone, I was happy to donate them. I don't know if they're worth anything or not, but that's for you to find out, right?"

"Yes, it is. I'm curious about the corner markings on the quilts. Do you know who made the quilts?"

"I have no idea. My mother was very protective of them. But she was always a little… off."

"She never mentioned where they might have come from? If she bought them, or if someone gave them to her?"

"No, but then she never said much to me. I left home when I was a teenager and we hadn't spoken since. Then I got a call that she was dying, so I did my duty and came back here to make final arrangements. Once she passed, I emptied the house. That trunk was the only thing that didn't go in the estate sale, so I donated it to the museum. I want nothing to do with it, those quilts, or anything that has to do with my mother."

"I'm sorry; this must be very difficult for you. I don't mean to upset you."

"It's all right, but I donated it for a reason. I want everything about that part of my life in the past. If you really want to know more about it, you could try contacting her sister, Audrina Bell. She is still pretty with it, as far as I know, and she might know more about the quilts."

"Thank you, I'll do that. I appreciate your help."

"I understand you have a job to do, but I really don't want to be involved with your research. Is that clear?"

"Yes, of course. I won't bother you again."

As she hung up the phone, Hannah wondered what could have happened between a mother and daughter that would lead to such animosity. Because she had been adopted, she often wondered about the biological connection between a mother and daughter. Though she adored and loved her own adoptive mother, she couldn't help but be curious if their own love and connection might be different or intensified somehow if they were biologically connected. Based on this conversation, it was clear that biology did not guarantee a bond.

As the day came to a close, she decided to take one last look at the quilts and resolved to try to locate Audrina Bell in the morning. When she stepped into the room where she had the quilts spread out, that scent greeted her again, only now it was peppered with the aroma of the quilts. She had yet to place exactly what it was. It seemed to have a flowery twinge, while still being rich and very familiar. She searched her memory, trying to figure out where she had smelled that in the past, but nothing came to her. She knew enough to let it go for now; her subconscious would continue to work on it, and those kinds of details often came back to her when she least expected it.

Before she had time to consider the action, her fingertips instinctively grazed the surface of the quilt. Her fingers tingled and her heart fluttered the moment she touched the cloth. Suddenly aware that she didn't have gloves on, she knew that she should pull her hand away, the oils from her skin could permanently damage the quilt. She knew better, yet she couldn't pull away. Her fingers traveled across the stitches, and her eyes fell shut. A soft hum began to brew deep in her throat. It was a song she'd hummed many times before, but she didn't know a single word, or where the melody even came from. As her fingertips continued along the quilt, she realized she touched each square in a certain order that seemed to correlate with the rise and fall of her humming. When the door to the processing room opened, she jolted out of her dazed state and drew her hand away.

"Hannah, what's going on?" Dr. Wagstaff reproached her.

"I'm... I'm sorry, Doctor, I don't know what came over me."

"You know better than to touch artifacts with your bare hands."

"I do, I'm so sorry. I guess I got caught up in the moment," Hannah offered. It sounded lame even to her ears, and she bit her lip at the look of consternation directed at her from Dr. Wagstaff.

"In this case, it's not... critical, it's not as if they are going on display. But please, Hannah, be more careful. Not following protocol is grounds to be terminated, and I would truly hate to lose you."

Her cheeks burned as she endured the criticism. Hannah knew that she was right; she'd made a foolish mistake. The thought of disappointing Doctor Wagstaff left her embarrassed and full of regret.

She'd admired Dr. Wagstaff's work at the museum ever since she was a young girl; her parents had brought her regularly to see the exhibits, and that influence was unmistakable in her life. During college, it became her dream to work for the museum, and in particular to work with Dr. Wagstaff. She couldn't believe she'd put it all at risk with something even the most novices in her field would avoid. What was she thinking?

"I'm very sorry, Dr. Wagstaff. It won't happen again."

"Please be sure it doesn't. You must be tired. Why don't you go home, and we'll get a fresh start tomorrow."

It was a statement, not a question. "Yes, of course."

She hurried past the doctor before Dr. Wagstaff could see the tears forming in her eyes. Hannah knew it wasn't just her mistake that upset her, it was the sensation of the quilt under her fingertips. It stirred something in her, something that she couldn't explain.

CHAPTER 2:

She woke early feeling exhausted after a restless night of tossing and turning from dreams that seemed vivid and real, yet just out of reach when she startled awake.

She chalked it up to worry. Would Dr. Wagstaff really forgive her for her mistake? Would it change how she respected her as an assistant, or impact her future at the museum? Why in the world had she even touched the quilt with her bare hands? She was always so careful and had never made a foolish mistake like that before.

It was as if something about the quilt made her mind so foggy that she didn't even hesitate to touch it. Maybe there was some kind of mold on it that she had inhaled? Maybe the scent that she breathed in so deeply had some kind of impact on her brain chemistry?

As much as she wanted to blame her actions on

something else, deep down she knew that there wasn't any real explanation for it. She had felt drawn to touch the quilt with her bare hands from the first moment she saw it—but why?

She was practically addicted to investigating old things, and had a knack for research and finding the truth and story behind the items she connected to, but this was the first time an object had influenced her this deeply.

As she prepared to leave for work, her anxiety turned to excitement; she could hardly wait to contact Audrina Bell and dig deeper into the history behind the quilts. She was a professional, and good at her job, and she wasn't going to let a momentary lapse shake her confidence. She decided to use the drive into work to try to think through her options, and by the time she arrived at the museum, a plan was beginning to form. She would begin by finding out what she could from Audrina, a thorough list of questions forming in her mind. She needed to find out as much as she could, or she would never be able to let go of the fascination she had with these quilts.

As soon as she was in her office she set her things down and picked up the phone to call Audrina. After the third ring, a frail voice answered. "Hello? Who is this?"

"Hello. My name is Hannah Quinn. I work for the Nelson-Atwell Museum, and I am trying to reach Audrina Bell. Is this Ms. Bell?"

"Yes, it is. But I don't have any money to donate, I'm sorry."

"Oh, I'm not calling for a donation. I'm calling about some items that were donated to the museum. They belonged, I believe, to your sister."

"I'm sorry, I don't know what you mean. My sister just passed away."

"Yes, and her daughter donated some of her things to the museum. An old trunk to be specific."

"What? She donated her trunk?" Her voice trembled as she spoke. "How could she do that? Was it empty?"

"I assure you, everything was legal about the donation."

"I imagine it was, but Delores should know better. Her mother would be heartbroken if she knew. That trunk was meant to stay in the family."

"I'm so sorry, Ms. Bell, but it was hers to donate, and she did. We found two quilts inside, and that's what I'm calling about."

"Yes, of course you did," her voice weary, resigned.

"Would you like me to look into whether you could claim the donation?" Hannah frowned. The last thing she wanted was to give up the quilts, but it was clear this woman was distraught that Delores donated them without thought.

"No, there's no reason for that. I don't have much longer on this earth myself, and I... well, I have no one to pass them down to. Will your museum put them on display?"

"I can't say for sure, but I do know they will be well taken care of, if that is any comfort."

"Yes, it is, thank you. They belong somewhere safe."

"Could you tell me a little bit about the quilts?"

"I don't know all there is to know, to tell you the truth. All I know is that they were handed down to my mother, and she told each of us that no matter what happened in our lives, they were to be kept safe and to be cared for."

"Did she make them?"

"No, Grandma Mary did. She wasn't my direct

grandmother, but that is how my mother always referred to her, so that was how we all thought of her. All I really remember hearing is that she made them as wedding gifts for her grandchildren, and I believe there were a dozen or so. I wish I had paid more attention to the exact details, but my sister and I were young girls when she passed away. We didn't care about quilts back then; we just wanted to honor her wishes."

"Did she ever tell you stories about them, or how they came to be?"

"Just that one quilt told the whole story, the sampler, and the other one was a piece of it. We always thought that there was some deeper story behind it, but neither of us ever had time to dig into it. However, I do know for certain that there are more quilts, and each mirrors one of the pieces from the sampler quilt."

"How do you know that?"

"One night, I was dreadfully sick. We lived on an isolated farm, and we got hit with an awful storm. There was no way to get me to the doctor or the hospital until the morning. Mother wrapped me up in the sampler quilt, and she told me that each one of the patches would give me the strength to get better. She said that even though my whole family couldn't be there to help me, I could still feel their love through the piece of the quilt that was theirs. I asked her what she meant, and she said that each piece represented another part of our family. At least, I think that was what she said; I was so ill, I couldn't think clearly. But that quilt made me so warm, and comfortable. I fell right to sleep. When I woke up the next morning, I was much better."

"What an amazing story. I would truly love to know

more about the quilts. Do you know of anyone else I can reach out to?"

"Perhaps you can do what we never had the chance to, and find the other quilts that were made. Maybe you can figure out the story behind them, and how they came to be passed down through our family. Beyond that, I'm afraid I can't help you."

"Would you like to help me do that?" Hannah asked.

"I'm afraid I can't. I'm too weak these days to do much of anything. But if you come across anything, I would love to know about it. Just promise me that you will take care of the quilts."

"Oh, yes, of course. The museum will take excellent care of them."

"No, I'm asking you, Hannah. These quilts have been passed from mother to child for generations. Unfortunately, my niece is not interested in family, and I have no one to give them to. I know I've never met you, but the quilts came to you for a reason. I'm asking you... will you please take care of them?"

"I will," Hannah whispered. Her heart ached at the loneliness in the woman's voice. "I will let you know as soon as I find anything out."

"Wonderful. Thank you so much. If there is anything else you think I can help you with, please feel free to call."

"Thank you." Hannah hung up the phone and grabbed a tissue to wipe her eyes. What was it about these quilts that made her so emotional? She'd been accused by past boyfriends of being too distant and detached, but for some reason, this woman's story moved her to tears.

CHAPTER 3:

Hannah knew she had to do whatever necessary to try to find all of the quilts. Perhaps if the story was intriguing enough, or if she could craft a story that was captivating enough, it would warrant putting them on display in the museum. That thought was all of the motivation she needed to get to work right away.

Her work as a curator meant she often had occasion to connect with genealogists. She sent an e-mail regarding the quilts to a friend from college, Callum Jones. Callum was an exceptionally good genealogist and detective—so good, in fact, that he often worked with different branches of the government on cases that warranted his expertise.

Next Hannah began researching databases on the two names she had. As she dug into Audrina Bell's past, she discovered her sister's name was Elizabeth. Their parents' names were Benton and Gretchen. Gretchen had a sister, named Marie, but that's where her tracking came to a stop. She couldn't find any record of Gretchen and Marie's parents or any additional siblings they might have had.

After hitting a roadblock with the names, she decided to study the embroidery on the large quilt instead. In the processing room, she took several pictures of each of the symbols on the quilt. Then she took a photograph of the symbol on the smaller quilt. As she worked, her cell phone buzzed in her pocket. She pulled it out to find a message from Callum.

Found some interesting history on your names. Lunch?

Sounds good, where?

He responded before she could put her phone down, the caf. my office.

Hannah hesitated. She didn't want to take up ten minutes of her lunch break on the walk to Callum's office, but she also didn't want to appear ungrateful, and she was more than a little curious. Sounds great. See you in an hour.

Hannah began to pace; physically moving her body seemed to help her put the pieces of her research puzzles together, but every time she walked by the quilts, her fingertips ached to feel the naked material beneath them again.

She grabbed her gloves and stood before the quilts, admiring them, willing them to help her find their story. She placed a gloved hand on each quilt, but the gloves seemed to block the sensations that almost vibrated from the material yesterday when she touched them with her bare hands, and although she knew she could not do that again, it was difficult to resist.

When she returned to her office, she uploaded the pictures of the embroidered sections on the quilt from her camera to her computer. Using the same program she used to analyze different languages, images, and artifacts, she ran the images. To her surprise, the program didn't find a single result. She decided to try to enhance the picture itself. Perhaps there was something more to be seen than the frayed surface of the quilt offered her. When she enhanced the picture, she discovered that what she thought were symbols, in some cases, actually appeared to be words. Due to the fraying, however, she found it impossible to piece together what the words were.

She bit her lower lip and sat back in her chair. Hitting roadblocks was one of the most frustrating things that she experienced in her work. The Internet had revolutionized the way research was done in the modern world, and more often than not she expected answers to be right at her fingertips. When they weren't, she grew both impatient and more intrigued. After more searching led to more dead ends, she glanced at her watch and realized that it was time to meet Callum. She grabbed her phone and walked through the museum toward the side exit.

CHAPTER 4:

When Hannah stepped inside the cafeteria, she spotted Callum right away. He was hard to miss with his thick red hair and broad shoulders; even sitting down he had a presence that was unmistakable. He seemed immersed in studying the papers splayed across the table in front of him.

Hannah paused, wanting to take him in for a few minutes, but he looked up and met her eyes—she felt a zing go right to her core, and when he smiled and waved her over, her stomach did a flip-flop. Her best friend Jessie told her that the reason she never truly warmed up to any of the other guys she dated was because of her crush on Callum, but until now, Hannah had always dismissed her teasing.

Although they shared several classes in common in college, their friendship had always remained just that—a friendship—and Callum had never indicated a desire for anything more.

When Callum cocked his head sideways and raised his eyebrows, Hannah tried to breathe through the butterflies and focus on the task at hand, the quilts.

"Hi, Callum," she greeted as she sat down across from him, and smiled as his sea-green eyes met hers.

"Hannah Quinn, you've brought me yet another challenge. I'm going to have to start charging you double."

"But you don't charge me at all," she grinned.

"Then double that. I mean it," he mocked in a gruff voice, moving his papers aside and grabbing the iPad off to his left. "I keep thinking that one of these days, you and I are just going to spend an afternoon hanging out, and doing zero research."

"Really?" Hannah asked, intrigued, deciding to play along. "You mean you actually have downtime between your full-time job and your consulting with the feds?"

"See, that's exactly what I mean." He smiled, and his eyes twinkled with laughter. "Maybe if we took our nose out of things long enough, we'd discover... the sky again."

She quickly glanced away, and felt his eyes seeking hers, but she didn't dare to meet them, instead, she fumbled with her camera and joked, "What? Are you telling me you've got an additional side-gig as a meteorologist? Do I sense a lecture on cloud formations coming?"

"Is that what you think? That I'm a know-it-all?"

"I hope that's what you are, because if I don't figure out this mystery, I'm going to lose my mind."

"Hmm, Hannah Quinn unhinged—now that's something I might want to see."

She should resist, really she should... "Why is that?"

"You're always so calm, so rational, Hannah. I can't quite imagine you otherwise."

"Ha, you've never seen me try to parallel park."

"Good point." He chuckled. "Let's get some food first, because neither of us is going to want to stop once we get started."

"I'm not hungry," she replied, reaching for his tablet.

"Watch it." He tugged it out of her grasp. "You have to eat, you know."

"I will, but right now I really just want to know what you've found."

"Okay, you take a look at this, and I'll grab us some food. Any preference?"

"You know what I like. Thanks." She risked eye contact and was rewarded with a dazzling smile that reached from his eyes, across the space between them, and all the way down to her toes. He slid the tablet over to her side of the table and walked away.

Breathe, just breathe, Hannah. Keep it cool.

As she began to go through the family tree he'd created on the tablet, she saw exactly what he found so interesting. Although there were several branches, there was a large gap in detail exactly where she was stuck. However, there were notes on the margin of the screen.

"The absence of records indicates that there may have been some scandal connected to this family."

Hannah jumped, unaware he had walked up behind her.

"Jeez, Callum. Give a girl some warning next time. So, what kind of scandal?"

"Oh, sorry." He set a plate with a veggie sandwich down,

along with a bottle of orange juice, and sat beside her rather than across from her. "Well, I'm not sure yet. During this period, there was a lot of flawed record keeping. However, sometimes people used that to their advantage. If, let's say, a child was born out of wedlock, that child may not have ever been documented, and in a sense, may not exist at all. But that child may still go on to create a family line of his or her own, with no roots to connect them back to an earlier time."

"So, you're saying that's what might have happened here?"

"I don't really know yet. That's one possibility. Your best resource, in this case, is going to be talking to descendants if you can."

"But I don't have that option. The last woman to possess the quilt passed away just days ago, and her sister doesn't have any more knowledge than I've given you. The daughter wants nothing to do with any of it."

"What a shame." He shook his head. "It's hard to see family lines end like that."

"Do you really think we've hit an end? I find it hard to believe, in light of all the information available today online. How can we both hit a dead end?"

"Well, you're right, it is rare to truly hit the end of a family line, but, yes, it can happen. In some cases, it only ends because the extended family has become so disconnected, they have no idea about one another. In that case, it's not so much that it's ended, as it is that it's forgotten."

"Like mine." She stared down at the tablet.

"What do you mean?" His eyes bore into hers when she glanced up.

"I don't have a family line."

"Hannah, what do you mean? I traced it for you in college, remember?" His brow furrowed as he took a bite of his sandwich.

"No, you traced my parents' history, Callum."

"Sorry, you lost me, Hannah. I'm not following…"

She studied him for a moment. She didn't tell very many people the truth about her history for two reasons. One, she was a very private person, and two, she never wanted her parents to think that she didn't consider them her real family.

Callum set his sandwich down and wiped his hands. "What is it, Hannah? You can tell me."

"I'm adopted." She smiled. "So, yes, I have a family history, through my parents—but it's not a biological history."

"Oh, wow! You never told me." He grinned. "How exciting."

"Exciting?" She laughed. "I didn't expect that reaction."

"You have a true mystery in your past. If it's something you're interested in, that is. It would be a lot of fun to trace it. Do you know anything about your birth parents?"

"Nothing. No one does, actually."

"Surely there are some records somewhere. Adoption papers, birth records?"

"No, not at all. I was found at five, abandoned. I was never reported missing, and there was no match to my DNA in the system. The only thing I knew, according to my mother, was my first name, Hannah."

"How interesting. It's good that they didn't try to change your name. You have some of your identity to hold on to."

"Maybe, or maybe I had a dog named Hannah, and me

as a kid thought it was my name. Or maybe it was Anna, but I heard it as Hannah. No matter what, it's not my identity. My identity is as the daughter of my parents."

"Sure, it is." He nodded. "But you must wonder."

"Sometimes." She looked down at the photograph on her camera. "Sometimes things have a deeper meaning to me, one I can't explain. Then I wonder if it has something to do with my early childhood."

"Do you remember anything?"

"Nothing." She shook her head. "The therapist I saw when I was a child said that the trauma of being abandoned may have blocked my memory, or I may have simply been too young to retain much."

"What do you think?" He reached out and took the camera from her hand. She tried not to think about the way his fingertips brushed against hers.

"I don't know. I guess I don't think about it that much. When I was little, I used to imagine all kinds of fanciful things. Embarrassing things." She blushed as she laughed.

"What kinds of things?" He skimmed through the pictures on the camera.

"Childish things. You know, that maybe I was a long-lost princess that had been smuggled to safety, or a movie star's kid. That kind of thing."

"A princess, huh?" He glanced up and smiled. "I could see that."

"Stop." She rolled her eyes. "Anyway, my mystery isn't what we're looking into today. I want to know more about the history behind these quilts."

"These images are interesting. Have you noticed the way that some of these look like words?" he asked, clearing his throat.

"Yes, but I can't make out the letters. I tried enhancing the photograph on my computer, but it only makes the letters more blurry."

"Interesting. I wonder if they could be places? Or maybe names?"

"I would guess names, possibly. Look at this." She pointed to the picture of the smaller quilt. "The design in the center, here, has the same shape as the name in this square." She showed him on the image of the larger quilt. "So, if they are names, then it's likely this quilt was made for a certain person, and that there will be a quilt made for the rest of the names, as well."

"Good find. You've got great detective skills. Well, from what I found in my digging around, many of the women in this family were seamstresses or involved in sewing of some kind. So, it would not surprise me if the quilts were made my hand by someone in the family line."

"I believe they were all made by one person."

"All?"

"Twelve, plus the sampler quilt."

"Wow, that would be a lot of work for one person."

"Yes, it would. I can't help but wonder where the rest of the quilts are. I think if we can pin down where they are and maybe even get to all of them, they would make a remarkable exhibit for the museum."

"Yes, I've heard that the museum is at risk of being closed this year."

"I don't even want to think about it. I have no idea what I'd do with myself if I couldn't work here."

"I'm sure there are other museums that would love to

have you."

"But this is where I want to be." She frowned. "I'm hoping we'll find a way to save it. Maybe enough people would be interested in these quilts—if we can find all of them—to generate some good income."

"That's a big wish to make on some old blankets, Hannah. I just don't want you to be disappointed."

"All I can do is try, right?"

"Right. So, here is where I think you should start." He pointed to a name on his tablet. "Audrina's mother, Gretchen, supplied uniforms to this private school." He pulled up the name of the private school on the screen. "The private school was owned by Josiah Ridge, and is still open, and run by his great-grandson, Jefferson Ridge. It's possible that the families were close at one time, as most women were not employed then. For Gretchen to have supplied the uniforms, she may have been doing it as a favor to Josiah, in which case Jefferson Ridge may still have some information about Gretchen and Benton that could provide us some guidance as to who their parents were, or where they might have come from."

"Wonderful, Callum! You really are amazing."

"Am I?" He smiled as he picked up his tablet. "Does that mean you'll let me come with you?"

"Aren't you too busy for that?"

"Not for a mystery like this. You know my weakness is for a good treasure hunt."

"Mine, too." She grinned. "Okay." She glanced at her watch. "I might be able to get away with a road trip tomorrow if I get the rest of the paperwork on my desk done today. Are you available tomorrow?"

"Sure. I'll pick you up."

"Maybe I should drive."

"No way—I'll pick you up." He stood up from the table.

"Um. It's technically my project and I'm a good driver." She stared up at him.

"Didn't you just tell me that you couldn't parallel park?"

She bit her lip to suppress a smile. "That has nothing to do with my driving."

"If you say so." He laughed. "Should I pick you up at the museum or your house?"

"The museum," she sighed. "I'll text you later to confirm in the event I can't get off work for some reason."

"Okay, great. Eight?"

"Eight is good."

"See you then."

CHAPTER 5:

Back in her office, Hannah took the time to jot down her thoughts after her conversation with Callum. If there was a scandal that erased the history of the quilts, she wondered if they would be able to overcome it. This was one of the reasons why she always wrote down her thoughts and took copious notes—the knowledge that people and things could be completely erased if proper documentation wasn't followed was something she'd experienced more than once.

A knock on the door of her office drew her attention.

"Yes?"

"Hannah, I was looking for you earlier." Dr. Wagstaff stepped inside and closed the door behind her.

"Is something wrong?" She could tell from the crease of her superior's brow that this was all business.

"I know I told you that you could look into the quilts, but I need you on another project."

"Oh, but I was just going to—"

"Hannah, if we don't come up with something to keep these doors open, we're going to have to close by the end of the year. One of the museums in the next state has offered to loan us their exhibit of precious gems, and I'm hoping it will drum up enough attention to get us by for a few more months. I need you to go there and coordinate this with their assistant director, then organize and promote the exhibit."

"It's possible that I could find all of the quilts that go with this set, and we could use it as a historical exhibit—"

"Possible won't keep the doors open. Get the exhibit set up, and if there is time after that, you can go back to the quilts. They're not going anywhere."

"Yes, you're right. I'm sorry. I will contact the museum about the gems right away."

"Thank you, Hannah." She paused beside the door and looked back. "I know that you are passionate about things, and I'm sorry for putting on the brakes, but right now all of our focus needs to be on generating funds. Okay?"

"Yes, Dr. Wagstaff, of course." She closed the pictures of the quilts on her computer and looked up the details on the museum. Before leaving work that night, she sent Callum a text to cancel their road trip.

Over the next few weeks, she focused on gems, how best to light and display them, how to maximize PR for the show, and how to ensure their security. Yet at the end of every night as she closed her eyes, the embroidery on the quilts floated back into her mind. She thought about the promise she made to Audrina, and she longed for the truth behind the mystery that the old trunk had brought into her life.

When she walked into her office after the first day of the gem exhibit, she found a small package on her desk. When she picked it up, she noticed that the return address belonged to Audrina Bell. With a buzz of excitement, she grabbed her scissors to carefully open the package. Flipping back the box top, she pulled out the contents. Her heart lurched at the sight of a small notebook. It was leather bound and appeared to be very old. On top of it was a folded letter from Audrina.

Dear Hannah,

I discovered this in my things. I had forgotten all about it. My mother gave it to me when I was young. I'm not sure that it will help you with the quilts, but I do hope that it might. I hope you are well. Thank you for doing what I do not have the strength to do.

Kind regards,

Audrina

She carefully lifted the book, turning it slowly from side to side. The scent of musty leather filled her nostrils. Under her fingertips, the texture of the cover stirred a brief sense of recognition, similar to her experience with the quilts.

When she opened the book to the first page, her eyes widened at the sight of a pencil sketch. It was the face of a small child with a wide smile. The artwork was quite skilled, and despite the age of the paper, it had been well preserved. As she continued to look through the book, she discovered that each page contained a portrait. Many of the faces were similar. Some, she thought, could have been older versions of others. It seemed like a photo album, perhaps created before photo albums were possible.

The only way to tell for sure was to date the paper; however, she knew the moment that she turned the notebook over to Dr. Wagstaff, it would become a possession of the museum. She didn't want to let go of it just yet. Audrina had sent it to her with the hope that she would be able to use it to find out more about the quilts. She tucked it safely away back in the box.

That night as she closed her eyes, she could see the faces in the sketches as they danced before her eyes. Who were these people? Who had drawn them? Were they related? The questions jammed up in her mind. She grabbed her phone and sent a text to Callum.

Road trip tomorrow?

After glancing at the clock, she wondered if it might be too late for him to answer. A second later she received a response.

Pick you up at eight.

She smiled to herself as she let her head rest on the pillow. Tomorrow was her first day off after working for weeks without a break, and with the gem display already set up, and security in place, she wouldn't be needed at the museum.

Tomorrow belonged to her, Callum, and the quilts. Could it be she would discover more of their story?

CHAPTER 6:

The next morning Callum was at her door at 8 AM sharp. She provided him with a cup of coffee-to-go, then settled into the passenger seat of his car. Just like Callum, everything about his car was in order. It was so clean she might have guessed it was brand new. His cell phone had a place, as did his briefcase, as did his sunglasses, and two granola bars.

"Breakfast," he smiled. "Because I've noticed that when you are consumed in a project, you forget to eat."

"Rather observant, aren't you?"

"I'd better be." He winked at her then started the car. As they drove, she told him about the notebook that Audrina sent. "Do you think it could help us in our search?"

"I'm not sure, to be honest. It would be difficult to pin down who the people in the sketches were when so much time has passed. However, it could have some historical value if we find out who drew them."

"I hope that we can."

"Me, too, Hannah."

In the almost three hours that passed, they discussed what it would be like to find the history and story behind the quilts, and what it might mean for the museum. Then they veered off into amusing memories of their time in college together. They were almost to their destination when Callum looked over at her.

"I was always trying to get your attention, you know. All of those ridiculous things I did—you must have thought I was a fool."

"My attention? You always had everyone's attention." She shook her head. "I never thought you were a fool, Callum."

"No?" He pulled into the parking lot of the private school.

"No, never." She smiled at him.

"Then why didn't you ever talk to me? I mean really talk to me. Every time I tried to get you into a conversation, you would find an excuse to get away."

"Oh, well." She picked at the edge of her shirt. "I was shy."

"Shy?" He laughed. "Now that I don't believe. I saw you go toe-to-toe with our professor in front of our entire Lit class."

"Because he insisted that the Nelson-Atwell Museum was nothing but old relics and dust. He was such a jerk."

"You let him know it, too."

"We should go in." She glanced at her watch. "It's lunch time, and I called ahead to let them know we would be here, so we should be able to get a good amount of time with Jefferson."

He stepped out of the car. When she joined him on the walkway that led up to the school, she wondered whether some of his friendly banter was hinting at something more. It was hard for her to believe, as she had never considered herself attractive.

She pushed the thought aside and focused on the man that stood at the front door of the school.

"Hello, welcome." He smiled at them both. "Was it a difficult drive?"

"Not at all." Hannah shook his hand. "I'm Hannah Quinn and this is the friend and expert I told you about, Callum Jones."

"Hannah, Callum, it's a pleasure to meet you. I hear that you're on the path of a historical discovery."

"I hope so." She smiled.

"Do come inside. The kids are at lunch so it may be a bit noisy, but my office should be quiet enough for us to talk."

As they walked down the halls of the school, Hannah flashed back to her own youth. Her parents were wealthy and she'd been provided with a private school education. She made every dime worthwhile by gobbling up all the knowledge she could. However, that alienated her from most of her peers, who were more interested in partying and skipping class. It wasn't until college that she truly bonded with a small group of friends.

Once they were settled in Jefferson's office, he lifted a box and set it on his desk. "My father was a big history buff. When you mentioned Gretchen, I did some digging, and I found a record of her making uniforms for the school.

According to the documentation at the time, she was a close friend of my great-grandmother."

"Is there anything in your documentation about Gretchen's parents? Or where she might have come from?"

"Yes, a few notes. Gretchen was taking care of her elderly mother, by the name of Mary, and as it is stated in these documents, she was named after her own mother. So, Gretchen's grandmother would have been Mary, as well. In order to get the job as seamstress for the uniforms, Gretchen claimed that her grandmother was an extremely skilled seamstress who had connections with royalty. She couldn't prove that, as her grandmother had no actual record of birth. But the name she gave, that she claimed belonged to her grandmother, was Mary Alice Godwin Benton Palmer." He chuckled. "Quite a mouthful, right?"

"Yes, it is, and exactly what we needed to hear. Thank you so much for this, Jefferson. Do you think it will be enough for you to find out more about the family, Callum?"

"Yes, I do. With that many surnames, I should be able to track everything. Did you have any other information about Gretchen or her family?"

"Only that there was some kind of scandal in their past. My great-grandfather made a note in his personal diary, that the story of Gretchen's family was almost unbelievable, but that she was a good and honest woman. He believed what she said, but whatever it was, he didn't commit it to paper. That in itself tells me that it was big, as he normally documented everything. If he didn't write this down, then he likely considered it too much of a risk to mention on paper."

"How very interesting." She smiled. "Who knew a search

for quilts would lead to such intrigue?"

"I still have a few of the uniforms that Gretchen made on display in the school's museum. She was an excellent seamstress, and the uniforms were flawless. You're welcome to take a look, if you would like."

"Thank you so much." She smiled as she stood up, and then nodded. "I appreciate all of your help with this."

"No trouble at all. This school owes a great debt to Gretchen's family. If there is anything more I can do to help, please feel free to ask." He shook her hand, then Callum's.

After he directed them to the small room that served as the school's museum, Hannah stepped inside to take a look around. Callum followed after her, but he already had his tablet out.

"Look at this, Callum." She pointed out the uniforms behind a glass case. "Even if she was the best seamstress in the world, do you really think that someone would go to all of the trouble of encasing the uniform?"

"I don't know; I guess it would depend on how valuable I thought the uniforms were. As Jefferson said, his great-grandfather was an avid historian."

"Yes, and he knew something about Gretchen's family, something that he didn't dare write on paper. Maybe that something influenced him to take even more precautions with preserving the uniforms."

"You mean, he thought they might be worth a lot of money some day?"

"Yes, maybe."

"I'm not sure. It's a long shot."

"You said yourself that the bloodline ended for a reason, that there may have been a scandal in the family. Obviously, that was most likely the case, as it's been confirmed by the distinct lack of documentation."

"Sure, but we don't know what. I mean, it could have been very simple. Back then, their moral standards and extensive restrictions on women allowed for many things to be scandals that wouldn't even be thought of twice now."

"I just think it's something we should look into."

"Absolutely." He met her eyes. "I just don't want you to be disappointed if it turns out not to be what you're expecting."

"Why do you always do that, Callum?" She turned to face him.

"What?"

"You're always saying you don't want me to be disappointed. Like somehow it's your job to prevent that."

"I'm sorry, I didn't mean to upset you."

"No, I'm not upset. I'm just curious."

"I don't want you to be hurt, Hannah."

"But it's not your job to protect me." She shrugged. "I can take the risk of believing in miracles, can't I?"

"You can, but," he cleared his throat, "I've never seen one myself."

"Well, buckle in, Callum, because if you stick with me, you're going to see one, or two, or three or more."

"You really believe that much?" He raised an eyebrow.

"The only way to create a miracle is to believe. There are no other options to save the museum, so yes, I'm going to believe. I'm not asking you to, but I am asking you not to try to protect me anymore. I want to take the risk."

"All right." He smiled. "Then I'll do my best to believe with you. Let's go get some lunch, and I'll look over what I've found so far."

"Sounds good." She led the way back to the car. As she snapped her seat belt into place, she glanced over at him. It meant a lot to her that he wanted to protect her, but what did that mean, exactly?

CHAPTER 7:

"This is very interesting." Callum skimmed through some results on his tablet. "Based on the information that Jefferson gave us, I think I've found Mary."

"What? Really?" Hannah leaned over to look at the tablet and nearly knocked his elbow off of the table.

"Okay, slow down." He laughed and pushed the tablet toward her. "See for yourself."

"Mary—had four children and twelve grandchildren. This must be her! How did you find her?"

"Once I had her name, it wasn't too hard. Although there are no birth records for her, there was a death record. Once I had that, I could find the survivors, and that led me to the others."

"So, we still don't know exactly who Mary was?"

"Not exactly, but I'm going to look into it more.

Meanwhile, you have a solid trail to follow, don't you think?"

"Wow, I can't believe it. You're an amazing researcher, Callum."

"You think so?" He sat back and Hannah felt his eyes, unblinking, zoomed in on her. Her cheeks felt warm, and her breath caught in her throat.

Redirect, Hannah, just redirect…

"Yes, I know so. I can't wait to call Audrina and tell her about this. To think those quilts have survived so long, it's astonishing. Now, if we can trace the other grandchildren, then we might be able to find the other quilts. Provided they are still out there somewhere and in decent condition."

"It's important to consider that not every family may have been so careful with their quilts." He frowned. "Sorry, there I go again."

"Don't be. You're right. It's a bit much to expect that they'll all be in perfect quality. But I'm going to try. It seems, at least from what I've learned thus far, that the quilt recipients felt there was something very special about them, and that they needed to keep them safe, so we have that going for us."

On the drive home, Hannah kept her gaze trained to the side window; her mind was a million miles away.

In her mind, she could see herself at the foot of Grandma Mary's rocking chair, gazing up at her with adoration as she worked on her quilts. Whoever Grandma Mary was, she must have loved her family very much to invest so much time in creating such beautiful and intricate quilts.

Maybe that was the sensation she felt when she touched the quilt—the power of love, as it traveled through the years.

When Callum turned into the parking lot of her apartment building, she came back to the present as he put the car in park.

"I'll walk you up to the door."

"No, you don't have to do that, Callum. I'm good."

"I want to. I mean, if you don't mind." He offered a half-quizzical smile.

"Sure, I guess." She stepped out of the car, and he followed after her.

"This is a nice building."

"It was in my price range." She shrugged. "It serves its purpose, considering I'm not here all that much."

"Now you sound like me."

"Heh, I guess I do."

He felt warm and strong beside her; it felt natural. That realization made her drop her keys as she fidgeted with the lock on her door, their heads almost hitting as they both reached down to pick them up.

"Hannah?"

"Y... yes?" she stammered as she put all her attention on the lock.

"If you'd like, I can look into your past, as well. I wasn't sure if I should offer. I wasn't sure how you would feel about it. But I might be able to find something that would be helpful to you."

"How?" She brushed her hair back from her eyes and studied him. "There's absolutely no record of me."

"There was no record of Grandma Mary, either. But I found her." He reached out and swept her blonde bangs away from her eyes, tucking them behind her ear, and she felt the draw of his eyes on hers. "Your eyes are the most unusual shade of blue, Hannah. Startling. There are always clues. I can find you, too."

"I'm... I'm right here." Her cheeks grew hot. Could he see the blush in them? Was she reading too much into this? "I mean, finding my past, I don't think it will change much," she countered as she pushed her door open.

"Maybe not. But knowing your roots might let you put down some of your own."

She turned back to him. "You think I don't have roots?"

"I think you live in an apartment, in your price range, that serves its purpose, and are willing to give every ounce of your time and energy to save a museum that you consider to be your home. I think maybe you're afraid to put down roots, because even though you had an amazing family, a part of you still feels like it is lost."

She gripped the doorknob tight. "I never thought of it that way. But, well, I don't know. Let me take some time to think about it, okay?" She risked looking into his eyes. They were mere inches from her own, and she knew in that moment that he could see right through her—her uncertainty, fears, and maybe even her love—bare before him.

His eyes brightened, as though he had found hope after a long drought.

He held her gaze for a moment, then nodded. "You know where to find me. I'll see you soon, Hannah."

"I do," she whispered, walking through the door and closing it behind her, leaning against it for support. Was Callum interested in her, or was he simply interested in solving another mystery— her mysterious past?

Callum's family was well-to-do; his father was a senator, and his mother volunteered with several non-profit organizations locally. He had roots, deep and solid, and connections beyond anything she had ever known.

He couldn't be interested in her—she must be reading into it. Her emotions had been all over the place since she started working with the quilts. He's just interested in helping her solve another mystery, and maybe that was enough. She doubted he would be able to find anything, but she was willing to let him try.

Pulling her phone out of her pocket, she texted: Go for it.

Within two seconds her phone buzzed, On it.

Moments later, Hannah settled on the couch and dialed Audrina's number. It rang several times before someone answered.

"Hello?" The male voice was abrupt.

"Hi, I'm trying to reach Audrina Bell?"

"I'm sorry, she's already gone."

"Gone?" She held her breath.

"To the hospital. Are you a friend of hers?"

"Sort of. Is she ill?"

"She will likely be passing in the next day or two. The doctors are just making her comfortable."

"Oh no, how terrible—and her sister just died."

"They were very close. As much as it hurts to lose them, it seems fitting that they go so close together."

"Would you tell me what hospital she's in?"

"She's unable to talk, but they are allowing friends to visit."

"All right, yes, I'll do that." Her heart raced as she jotted down the name of the hospital and Audrina's room number.

Suddenly she knew exactly what she had to do. But could she really go through with it?

CHAPTER 8:

The sun was setting as she approached the museum. Her heart fluttered in her chest. She was certain that she shouldn't go through with what she'd planned, but for some reason, she just couldn't resist. She used her key card to enter the museum and nodded to the night security guard.

He was accustomed to seeing her come in and out of the museum at all times of the day and night. She let herself into the processing room and opened the trunk. Without the slightest hesitation, she lifted the quilt out of the trunk and held it close to her. There it was, she'd already done it. She'd already touched it without gloves. What difference did it make if she went a few steps further now?

The vision of Grandma Mary carefully sewing the patches of the quilt together, in the hope that the quilt would keep someone she loved warm, filled her. Audrina was one of her descendants, and this quilt belonged to her family, even if it was donated to the museum.

Hannah tucked the quilt carefully into her bag, then turned and carried it out of the museum. The bored guard had barely offered her a nod.

As she drove to the hospital, she reviewed all the rules she'd broken. If Dr. Wagstaff found out, she would fire her on the spot. And yet for some reason, that wasn't the most important thing to her; it didn't even matter anymore.

The desire to see Audrina, and let her hold the quilt one last time, was more powerful than anything else she considered.

Once she arrived at the hospital, she hesitated as she walked down the hall. What if the hospital staff didn't allow her to see Audrina? But the woman at the nurse's desk smiled, almost as if she recognized her. "It's wonderful to see family, finally. We were hoping she would have visitors."

Hannah cleared her throat and considered correcting her, but that would only prevent her from getting into the hospital room, so she played along.

When she reached the door of Audrina's room, she noticed an elderly man sat beside the hospital bed. The woman in the bed was pale, and Hannah wondered if she were still alive.

"Oh, hello. I'm sorry, am I interrupting?"

The man stood up as he stared at her.

"What is it?" She stared back at him.

"You're the woman I spoke to on the phone? I recognize your voice."

"Yes, I am."

"I'm so glad you're here."

"I just felt it was best if I brought this to Audrina." She pulled the quilt from the bag and walked up to the side of the bed.

"Audrina?" Hannah whispered softly, "I don't know if you remember speaking to me on the phone, about the quilts. But I just want you to know that I found Grandma Mary, and I'm going to find all of her grandchildren and all of her quilts. I promise, I will make sure they are all where they belong. Including this one." She spread the quilt out over Audrina's body, and placed it under her hands. As she did, a tear trickled down one of Audrina's eyes. It made their faded blue shade seem to glow for a moment.

Hannah slipped her hand into Audrina's and held it gently, tears streaming down her face. "I'm sure that Grandma Mary would have wanted you to have it, and to know that it will be kept safe."

"I'm sorry, she hasn't been able to talk since she collapsed yesterday. I'm sure she appreciates it, though." The man beside her bed continued to stare at Hannah with wide eyes. She guessed he was touched by the effort she'd made to bring the quilt to Audrina.

"It's okay, you don't have to talk, Audrina. Just rest. I'll sit with you, if that's okay?" She sat down in the chair beside her bed and continued to hold her hand. Audrina squeezed her fingers just ever so faintly, but enough for Hannah to know she was listening. "I don't know what it is about these quilts, but they are so beautiful. I'm really glad that I had the chance to see them, and to find you." With her free hand, she traced her fingertips along the pattern of thread on the square closest to her. "I hope it gives you some comfort to have your sister's quilt with you."

Audrina lifted her head some and looked into Hannah's eyes. "It's… yours," she whispered. Her hand lovingly swept over the quilt and back to Hannah's hand. "Y… yours."

"Oh, thank you, Audrina. I will make sure the museum takes good care of it." She decided not to add that she would do it personally. She might not even work at the museum after this.

"No," the man insisted, "she's telling you it's yours. It belongs to you. What did you say your name was?"

"Hannah, my name is Hannah Quinn." She studied him for a moment. With the way he looked at her, she wasn't sure she should have given him her last name.

"Hannah." He closed his eyes and nodded, and something Hannah could not identify flickered across his face. Then he tilted his head toward the photographs on the table beside Audrina's bed. "I brought these here because I didn't want her to feel alone."

"Oh? Is it her family?" Hannah smiled. "What a lovely idea," she affirmed, leaning toward the photos. She skimmed the faces in the frames until she came to one that looked almost exactly like her.

"What?" Hannah stammered. Audrina's hand tightened on Hannah's again. "H- how is that possible?"

Hannah glanced at the look-alike photo again. Now she understood why the nurse thought she was family; she also realized that Audrina had the same unusual shade of blue eyes that she did. Everyone commented on Hannah's eye color when they met her—they were a cross between faded blue and gray, depending on the light and what she was wearing that day. She had never met anyone with her same color eyes—until now.

"Audrina had a daughter." He lowered his eyes for a moment. "We had a daughter." When he looked back up at Hannah, his cheeks were bright red. Her stomach clenched; she felt suspended between dread and something she couldn't identify.

"We were just kids, we weren't married, and when we found out, we went to Audrina's father—but he refused to let her marry me. So her parents sent Audrina away and then gave the baby to a family friend after she was born. But Audrina couldn't bear to be apart from her. She tried to be part of her life as much as she could be, but then when the—our child became an adult, she got herself into some trouble. She was lost, had a hard life, we tried to help her, but she refused. And then she had a baby. A little girl."

He swallowed hard, lifting his eyes from the floor to Hannah's. "She dropped the baby off with Audrina because she couldn't be a mother. We were grateful that she realized that, at least. Audrina was afraid that the baby would be taken away from us if anyone knew, so she kept the baby a secret. She only told me, and her sister. The baby was about five when Audrina's niece found out. She threatened to go to the police. Audrina was afraid that if she did, the child would be given back to her mother, who was involved in drugs, or even end up a ward of the state.

"Before that could happen, she researched the best possible adoption agencies, and took the baby—she took you—there."

"What? Me?" Hannah shook her head. "This is crazy. It's not possible."

"It is." He studied her intently. "I'm so sorry that we

couldn't do more for you. I was going to fight for you, but then you were adopted by a great couple, and I was so old already, I just thought it would be better to let you have your life with a young couple who couldn't have children of their own."

"Audrina?" She looked back to her. "Is this true? Are you my grandmother?"

"It's yours." She tapped the quilt. Hannah closed her eyes and allowed her fingertips to trace the pattern on the quilt. All at once she realized that it wasn't just a sensation, it was a memory. When she imagined sitting at Grandma Mary's feet, it was actually Audrina she was picturing. When she opened her eyes again, tears spilled from her eyes.

Hannah felt frozen in time, but as she watched Audrina's face, she knew her time was short. There was only one thing left to do.

"I will take care of it, I promise." She leaned down and kissed Audrina's forehead. "I didn't forget you, Grandmother, please know that. I have always remembered your love."

CHAPTER 9:

Hannah espent the rest of the night, and well into the next morning, holding her grandmother's hand. Though it was hard for her to believe, she didn't question the connection she felt between herself and Audrina.

Around dawn, she stepped outside for some fresh air and found that she'd missed a call from Callum. She returned the call, and he answered on the first ring.

"Hannah, you're not going to believe this."

"I already know."

"No, wait, what? Listen to me, you're going to want to hear this."

"I know, Callum, Audrina is my grandmother."

"What? How do you know?"

"I came to see her last night, and when I did, I found out the truth. I'm still struggling to comprehend it, to be honest." Her voice wavered as she looked back at the hospital. "Callum, I remember her now and the quilts. She raised me for those first five years. I wasn't abused; I wasn't neglected. I wasn't unwanted. She gave me away because she wanted to protect me." Hannah whispered into the phone.

"Oh, Hannah, how are you handling it? Are you okay?"

"I'm not sure, to be honest. She's dying, and I desperately wish I had more time with her. I just want... more time."

"Where are you?"

"I'm at the hospital with her."

"Text me the name of the hospital, all right?"

"She might not be around long enough for you to send flowers."

"Just text me the name, Hannah, please."

"Okay, I will. Thanks for all of your help, Callum." She hung up the phone then sent the text. When she stepped back inside of the hospital room, she found that her grandfather was asleep on the chair beside Audrina's bed.

She stared at them, her grandmother covered up in the quilt made by Grandma Mary, and her grandfather beside her—both so frail, a reminder of how short and fleeting life could be.

Perhaps if her grandmother had been allowed to keep her, things would have been different. Or maybe they wouldn't have. She didn't really know how she felt about it all because she'd had adoptive parents who were loving and supportive, and she would not change that for anything. It was complicated.

Yet, Hannah was grateful that she had the chance to know the truth before her grandmother died. As she sat down beside her again, she thought about the other quilts that were still out there somewhere. They belonged to family—her family—to people that she would never have known existed.

As the hours slipped past, Audrina gradually stopped grasping Hanna's hand. She no longer lifted her head or opened her eyes. Hannah longed for a way to magically make her stay longer, but she knew that Audrina's body would give out. As her breathing grew faint, Hannah hummed the song that she had forgotten the words to. When her grandfather heard it, he began to sing softly.

"Softly sleeping, 'neath the love of those that left so long ago, softly dreaming 'bout the joy that only time can know, softly growing in the branches of an endless tree, rest now, little child, and remember to dream of me." He smiled as he held Audrina's other hand. "Your grandmother used to sing it to you every night, as her mother sang it to her, and probably her mother before her."

"I'll remember, Grandmother, I'll remember. Always." She squeezed her hand again, just as Audrina took her last breath, and peace flooded her face.

"I think she's gone," Hannah whispered, tears unbidden, streaming down her face.

A nurse and doctor rushed in, and Hannah was bustled out of the room, and right into the arms of someone standing just outside the door.

"Callum?" She stared into his warm green eyes as he wrapped his arms around her.

"It's all right, Hannah, I'm here," he comforted her as he led her to the waiting room.

She nestled into his grasp as the tears continued to flow. When they finally subsided, he offered her a tissue and a tender kiss on the top of her head.

"I'm so sorry, Hannah. I wish we had found her sooner."

"I know, Callum. Me, too."

"Hannah—" Callum and Hannah turned toward her grandfather as he sat beside her and placed his hand on her shoulder. "You gave her so much peace. You have to know that. She's spent her life wondering about you and wanting to see you again. This was the greatest gift you could have given her."

"Thank you." She wiped at her eyes. "But it's not the only gift I can give. I am going to make sure that every one of those quilts is found. I'm going to make sure that Grandma Mary's family has the chance to reunite again. It can't end here."

"I think that's wonderful. If there is anything I can do to help, all you have to do is ask." He offered her his hand. "I'm Benjamin, by the way."

"Benjamin, it's nice to meet you." She shook his hand, and then stood, pulling him in for a hug.

"Can you forgive me, Hannah? Forgive us?" He held her close.

"There's nothing to forgive, Benjamin. You and Audrina gave me a beautiful life. You did what you thought was right, and it was." She gazed into his eyes. "Now I have the chance to get to know you, and hopefully through you, Audrina."

"Yes, I would love that."

A nurse walked up to Hannah with the quilt folded in her hands. "I thought you might want this."

"Yes, I do. Thank you." She ran her fingertips along the patches and pulled the quilt to her chest. As hard as it was to lose Audrina, she had a promise to keep, and there was no time to spare.

As Callum and Hannah left the hospital together, he took her hand. "I'll drive you home."

"I have my car."

"I want to drive you." He brushed his fingertips along the curve of her cheek, which was still damp with tears. "You've been through a lot, Hannah. Let me see you home safely."

"What about your car?"

"I can find a way to get it home later. Don't worry about that now. I just want to make sure that you are okay."

"Always protecting me." She smiled through fresh tears.

"I always will, if you'll let me." He opened the car door for her. The words didn't set in until he was already behind the wheel and driving down the road. Were they meant in friendship? When she stole a glance over at him, she noticed his cheeks were flushed. Was he blushing?

They were a half-hour from home when her cell phone rang. The moment she saw the name, her heart dropped. "Hello, Dr. Wagstaff."

"Can you tell me why someone matching your description took something from the museum last night without authorization? I told security it couldn't possibly be you. I told them that you would never do that because it would be stealing. Please tell me I'm right."

"I'm so sorry, Dr. Wagstaff, I can explain."

"Put her on the speaker phone." Callum insisted.

"What, why?"

"Just trust me, she's going to want to hear this."

"Dr. Wagstaff, I have Callum Jones with me; he's been helping to trace the history and family line of the quilts. I'm going to put you on speaker phone, so you can hear what he has to say."

"Unless it's an explanation for you losing your mind, I'm not sure I want to hear it."

Hannah cringed as she pressed the speaker phone button.

"Hannah was able to verify, with the last living relative, the authenticity of the quilt. Which is going to mean a lot, when you put them on display in the museum."

"What do you mean? Why would I display the quilts?"

"We are on our way to the museum, Dr. Wagstaff, and I'll tell you in person. Are you available now?"

"I don't have time to waste on old quilts, Mr. Jones. Is this really important enough to meet in person?"

"Yes, Dr. Wagstaff, it is. We'll see you in ten minutes."

CHAPTER 10:

"Yes, it's true and verifiable with the documents I have uncovered, Dr. Wagstaff. These quilts were made by the illegitimate daughter of a prince whose name I guarantee you are going to know. Having just one of the quilts will be enough to generate funds for the museum, but if we can manage to get them all, it will save the museum not just for this year, but for the foreseeable future."

"This is just too incredible. Who is it? What's the name of the prince?"

"I'll provide you with all the documentation you need as soon as we have uncovered the other quilts, but until then, I suggest that you keep all of this information completely confidential. You can imagine what will happen if word gets out and competing museums try to find the other quilts first."

"Hannah, how long have you known about this?" Wagstaff asked, her tone slightly less hostile than it had been.

"I'm just finding out right now. I've been at the hospital saying goodbye to a—to my grandmother. Callum came by to share the news with me, but she died before he had the chance. Then you called, and well, the rest is history."

"Well, this is a lot to take in. Excuse me while I make a call to have additional security added to our night watch. Callum, I have your promise that this information will remain in the strictest confidence?"

"Yes, of course, Ms. Wagstaff. I consider myself to be working on Hannah's behalf, and thereby the museum's, as well."

"Very good. Hannah, why don't you take a few days off, and let's regroup on Monday, shall we?"

"Yes, of course."

"And Hannah, I'm sorry for your loss. I truly am."

Hannah fought back the tears that threatened to spill yet again. She managed to murmur, "Thank you."

CHAPTER 11:

"Callum, I have to be honest, if I didn't know better, I would think that was all a lie just to protect me."

At his look of shock, Hannah quickly clarified, hastening her steps toward the car. "Don't get me wrong, I know you would never lie, but I have to be honest—this is all a bit difficult to believe."

"I'm sure it is, and that's why I double and triple-checked my source; it's the truth. It looks like you weren't so far off with your childhood dreams of being a princess, Hannah. Several times removed now, but royal blood flows through your veins."

"That's incredible," she managed, leaning on the car for support.

"I still need to go through the official verification process, and in light of the fact that Grandma Mary was an illegitimate child, it's very possible it will remain buried, but it will be a lot easier to do that if we can find the rest of Grandma Mary's descendants, along with the quilts. We have a big job ahead of us." Their car doors closed in unison.

"We do?"

"We do. Partners?" He looked over at her and rested his hand on top of hers.

"Absolutely." She smiled in return.

"If we're going to be working together, I should confess something."

"Really? Do tell," she laughed, as he started the car and began backing out of the parking spot.

"Hannah Quinn, I've had a crush on you since college, and I'm tired of waiting for you to notice."

"Waiting for me to notice? Are you kidding?" She laughed, hopeful.

"I'm not kidding, and let's stop waiting." He pulled back into the nearest parking spot and shifted the car into park, then leaned across the seat and kissed her.

All the questions and thoughts of princes and princesses fled her mind, as the passion behind his kiss met its match. A blazing horn startled them both, as Malcolm slammed his car door, giving them two thumbs up on his way past the car.

Hannah grudgingly smiled through her embarrassment, suddenly aware of their joined hands, resting on Grandma Mary's quilt.

She couldn't help but wonder at the power of the quilt, created with so much love, so many lifetimes ago.

I hope you enjoyed this Prequel to the historical romance series, Grandma's Wedding Quilts. Please consider leaving a review on Amazon at KateCambridge.com/prequelreview, and share the book with your friends.

I've had many readers asking if there's going to be a sequel to The Prequel (yes, I know...) -- they want to know if the other quilts are found, and what happens with Hannah and Callum! Well, the sequel is coming soon, and I'm pleased to share that Hannah and Callum will be popping up in more books in the near future. Stay tuned on social media (@KateCambridgeAuthor) and join the CHOICE READERS UPDATES at KateCambridge.com/choice. You'll be the first to know.

Visit Amazon.com and search for **Grandma's Wedding Quilts** and you'll find all the books written in this series collaboration – the stories of the romances that inspired each of the quilts sewn by Grandma Mary. You won't want to miss even one! You can also find them all in one place by visiting: SweetAmericanaClub.com.

Turn the page to find a short excerpt from each story in the series.

THE GRANDMA'S WEDDING QUILTS SERIES

It's an honor to collaborate with all the women authors in the Sweet Americana Book Club, part of the Sweet Americana Sweethearts blog.

Please visit the Sweet Americana Book Club group page on Facebook to connect with each author and find out what's happening with new author series collaborations.

Grandma's Wedding Quilts - The Prequel #1 - Kate Cambridge

The greatest inspiration is often born of desperation.

One year ago Hannah Quinn scored her dream job, and now the fait of the museum she loves will rise or fall on her next exhibit. But wait... there's a problem. She doesn't have a clue what her next exhibit will be!

When a trunk with two quilts is donated to the museum, Hannah's boss thinks she's wasting her time chasing down the history of the quilts, regardless of their beauty; but Hannah persists. She knows there's something special about these quilts, and a story that demands to be told.

Little does Hannah know, her friend Callum, a researcher and consultant, plays an unexpected a role in her investigation that leads to questions *and discoveries that threaten the foundation of all she holds most dear.*

Will her desperation to discover the story of the quilts

cause her to lose the very thing she loves the most - or will the secrets she uncover lead her to more than she ever dreamed?
https://KateCambridge.com
Author Page:
https://www.amazon.com/Kate-Cambridge/e/B01BD3X4ZU

* * *

Kizzie's Kisses #2 – Zina Abbott

Running from hostile Indians attacking Salina, Kansas, feisty Kizzie Atwell runs into freighter Leander Jones traveling the Smoky Hill Trail. He is as interested in her as his stallion is in her mare. The two join forces to prevent the Fort Riley Army captain from requisitioning their prize horses for the cavalry. Will the bargain they make to save their horses lead to a more romantic bargain sealed with a kiss?
http://zinaabbott.homestead.com/
Amazon Page:
http://www.amazon.com/Zina-Abbott/e/B00OWRJ3R8/

* * *

Jesse's Bargain #3 – Kay P. Dawson

Thanks to a gunfight, Cora now needs to get to Kansas, and Jesse needs a new trail cook. Left with no other choice, she joins the cattle drive headed north, with a man who isn't happy to have her along. They have miles of trail ahead of them - and a lot that can go wrong along the way.
http://www.kaypdawson.com/
Amazon Page:
http://amazon.com/author/kaypdawson

* * *

Meredith's Mistake #4 – Amelia C. Adams

The summer Meredith turned eighteen was filled with romance and laughter - two young men sought her hand, and she chose the one she thought would make her the happiest. He certainly was the most handsome, and the wealthiest, and could offer her the most pleasant life. But that turned out to be a mistake . . . one she would regret for a very long time.

In a strange twist of fate, now she's being given a chance to set things right. Will she be able to live down her past, or will her foolishness keep coming back to haunt her and keep her from ever being happy with the man she loves?

www.ameliacadams.com

Amazon Page:

http://amzn.to/2kv1tRT

* * *

Monica's Mystery #5 - Kate Cambridge

Monica has to leave home, fast. Her parents are planning to marry her off and although all her friends are marrying, that is definitely not what she wants. She's an amateur sleuth, and sees no reason why she can't join the ranks of the local lawman, or even become a Texas Ranger, should she choose! What will happen when she visits her best friend in Texas, only to find herself face-to-face with a handsome Texas Ranger, and knee-deep in territory she has no idea how to navigate?

https://KateCambridge.com

Author Page: https://www.amazon.com/Kate-Cambridge/e/ B01BD3X4ZU

* * *

Pleasance's First Love #6 - Kristin Holt

His worst mistake was letting her go.

His second-worst mistake? Bringing her home.

No one will ever know how badly Pleasance Benton's abandonment threw Jacob Gideon. He landed hard, hard enough he didn't care to find a replacement. Now that he needs a woman, he figures the safest way is to order one from a catalog.

Pleasance is back to reclaim her rightful place at Jacob's side. One way or another she'll remind him theirs is a match made in heaven…once the shock wears off. The teensy-weensy problem? Jacob doesn't know that she—*his first love*—is his catalog bride.

http://www.kristinholt.com/

Amazon Page: http://amzn.to/2ccSQWR

* * *

Zebulon's Bride #7 - Patricia PacJac Carroll

He's vowed not to marry until he reaches Montana. Then he meets her, but she has other ideas.

Zebulon Benton dreams of going to Montana, but he's the only son and his mother doesn't want him to go and his father needs help with the family store. Unknown to Zeb, his mother sends off for a mail order bride. After all, if Zeb marries and settles down, he won't want to leave.

Enter Amy Gordon from New York. She appears to be the perfect bride for Zeb. Except she also wants to go to Montana and nothing is going to stop her especially her love for Zeb.

http://www.pacjaccarroll.com/

Amazon Page:

https://www.amazon.com/Patricia-PacJac-Carroll/e/B008R9JCN2/

* * *

Ione's Dilemma #8 - Linda Carroll-Bradd

Relocating from Des Moines to the Texas frontier brings more challenges than socialite Ione has ever faced. All she wants is to avoid scandal but local carpenter Morgan is intent on courtship.

www.lindacarroll-bradd.com

Amazon Page:

https://www.amazon.com/author/lindacarroll-bradd

***

Josie's Dream #9 - Angela Raines

Could Doctor Josephine (Josie) Forrester and Lawman William Murphy get past their beliefs about life and love and find the future they were meant to have?

Author Page: http://amzn.to/1I0YoeL

***

Chase's Story #10 - P. A. Estelle

Chase wanted no part of going to college or following in his father's footsteps and becoming a Doctor. His dream involved cattle and horses and he follows that dream to the Arizona Territory. One cold, rainy day his life takes a turn when he finds himself looking down the muzzle of a Colt Walker barely being held up by a woman who has been badly beaten along with her three-year old son. Will she be someone Chase could let into his heart or someone who could destroy his life?

http://www.pennystales.com

Amazon Page:

http://www.amazon.com/Penny-Estelle/e/B006S62XB

＊

Tad's Treasure #12 – Shanna Hatfield

Tad Palmer makes a promise to his dying friend to watch over the man's wife and child. Will his heart withstand the vow when he falls in love with the widow and her son?

https://shannahatfield.com

Amazon Page:

https://www.amazon.com/Shanna-Hatfield/e/B0056HPPM0

ALSO BY KATE CAMBRIDGE

This is Kate's first book in with the Sweet Americana Book Club authors. Please also check out her **Suffragette Mail-Order Brides Series.**

See all Kate Cambridge's books at:

KateCambridge.com

Suffragette Mail-Order Brides Series Books

(Each is written to be standalone, so you can read them in any order, although Beginnings is truly the beginning of the series and the catalyst behind Elizabeth's choice to start the Choice Brides Agency. If you can read them in order, please do.)

Book 1: Beginnings

Book 2: Elizabeth

Book 3: Margaret

Book 4: Susan

Book 5: Lydia

Book 6: Lucy

Individual Books (Part of the Sweet Clean Book Club.)

MAE'S CHOICE: A Sweet & Clean Historical Frontier Western Romance

Grandma's Wedding Quilts, Book 5, MONICA'S MYSTERY
Grandma's Wedding Quilts, The Prequel

* * *

ACKNOWLEDGEMENTS

I am grateful for my amazing husband — for his encouragement, support, humor, patience, and love. He is my favorite person on the planet. I am blessed.

* * *

If you don't want to miss even one of the sweet historical or sweet contemporary books yet to be released, please join the **CHOICE READERS** Updates at KateCambridge.com/choice where you'll be the first to know when a new book launches at a fabulous same-day special launch price, as well as notices of contests, ARC opportunities, and more!

LET'S CONNECT
KateCambridge.com/Facebook
Kate Cambridge.com/Instagram
KateCambridge.com/Twitter

* * *

EXCITING OPPORTUNITY
Send the link of your Amazon Review for any of Kate's books to:
katecambridgeauthor@gmail.com
and you can get a FREE review copy of her next book!

* * *

SUFFRAGETTES

The Women's Suffrage Movement impacted the rights and equality of women all over the world, and continues to impact women today. I am eternally grateful to the women who led this movement, at great sacrifice to themselves and those they loved; grateful to the men who supported them, and for the fact that **they never gave up** despite incredible adversity. May we never take that for granted.

~Kate Cambridge

Made in the USA
San Bernardino, CA
12 March 2017